450L

PALM BEACH COUNTY
LIBRARY SYSTEM
3650 Summit Boulevard
West Palm Beach, FL   33406-4198

Robin Hill School

The First Day of School

Written by Margaret McNamara
Illustrated by Mike Gordon

Ready-to-Read

Si   light
New York London Toronto Sydney New Delhi

For Becky & Chester and Michael & Cookie
—M. M.

SIMON SPOTLIGHT
An imprint of Simon & Schuster Children's Publishing Division
1230 Avenue of the Americas, New York, NY 10020
This Simon Spotlight edition June 2021
First Aladdin Paperbacks edition July 2005
Text copyright © 2005 by Simon & Schuster, Inc.
Illustrations copyright © 2005 by Mike Gordon
All rights reserved, including the right of reproduction
in whole or in part in any form.
SIMON SPOTLIGHT, READY-TO-READ, and colophon are registered
trademarks of Simon & Schuster, Inc.
For information about special discounts for bulk purchases, please contact
Simon & Schuster Special Sales at 1-866-506-1949 or
business@simonandschuster.com.
Manufactured in the United States of America 0521 LAK
2 4 6 8 10 9 7 5 3 1
Cataloging-in-Publication Data was previously supplied for the
paperback edition of this title from the Library of Congress.
Library of Congress Cataloging-in-Publication Data
McNamara, Margaret.
First day of school / Margaret McNamara ; illustrated by Mike Gordon. p. cm—(Ready-to-read)
(Robin Hill School) Summary: After a summer of playing with his puppy,
Charles is sad to learn that she cannot stay with him on the first day of school.
[1. First day of school—Fiction. 2. Schools—Fiction. 3. Dogs—Fiction.]
I. Gordon, Mike, ill. II. Title. III. Series. PZ7.M232518Fg 2005 [E]—dc22 2004016672
ISBN 978-1-5344-8536-5 (hc)
ISBN 978-0-689-86914-3 (pbk)
ISBN 978-1-4814-1065-6 (eBook)

Charles loved his puppy.

Her name was Cookie.

All summer long,

Charles played with Cookie.

They played catch.

They played ball.

They were always together.

On the night before
the first day of school,
Charles said to Cookie,

"Tomorrow we start first grade."

In the morning,
Charles walked to
Robin Hill School.

His mom and Cookie
came with him.

When they got to school,
Charles said to Cookie,
"Time to go to school!"

"Oh, Charles," said his mom, "dogs are not allowed in school."

"What?" said Charles.

"Nobody told me!"

He hugged Cookie tightly.

Mrs. Connor was the
first-grade teacher.
She saw how sad
Charles was.

"May I pet your dog?"
she asked.

"I guess," said Charles.

"He looks nice," said
Mrs. Connor.

"She is a she,"
said Charles.
"Her name is Cookie."

"I wish Cookie
could come
to school,"
he said.

"Me too," said Mrs. Connor.

"You do?" asked Charles.

"Oh, yes," said Mrs. Connor.

"If Cookie came to school,

she could live on the

playground.

She could sleep
in a cubby.

She would belong

to everyone

at Robin Hill School!"

Charles gave that
some thought.
"Mom," said Charles,
"you can take Cookie
home now."

Charles had a good
first day.

But he missed Cookie.

When the day was over,
Cookie was waiting for him.

She waited for him
every day,
because she was his dog.